E
Dou   Douglass, Barbara

Good as new

OEMCO

GOOD AS NEW

GOOD AS NEW

story by BARBARA DOUGLASS
pictures by PATIENCE BREWSTER

LOTHROP, LEE & SHEPARD BOOKS·NEW YORK

Library of Congress Cataloging in Publication Data
Douglass, Barbara, (date)   Good as new.   Summary:
When Grady's young cousin ruins his teddy bear,
Grandpa promises to fix the toy.   [1. Toys–Fiction.
2. Grandfathers–Fiction]   I. Brewster, Patience.
II. Title.   PZ7.D7479Go   [E] 80-21406
ISBN 0-688-41983-6   ISBN 0-688-51983-0 (lib. bdg.)

*This book is lovingly dedicated
to my grandfathers*
CLOUGH GAUNT
and
T. H. SEYMOUR

–B.D.

*For the grandfathers
of my children*
SPENCER HATCH BREWSTER
and
HOLLAND CHAUNCEY GREGG II

–P.B.

I thought my Grandpa could fix anything.
One morning last week he fixed
the hose and the fence,
and my swing and my sandbox,
and Yim Lee's fire engine, and Carmen's wagon.
But then my cousin K.C. came to visit
while Uncle Jonathan went riding with his club.
And K.C. started crying
as soon as my uncle rode away.

Nobody could make him happy,
not even Grandpa.
Because the only thing K.C. wanted
was my bear.
And I said, "Huh-uh.
Nobody plays with my bear but me."

K.C. kicked the floor and he cried some more
and Mom said, "Grady,
do you think K.C. feels lonely
because he didn't bring *his* bear?"
Then Dad said, "Do you think he might feel better,
son, if you just let him hold your bear?"

Grandpa didn't say anything, and K.C. cried even harder until
Yim Lee and Carmen grabbed their toys and went home.
Grandpa grabbed his hat and went for a walk.
And before I could say,
"Okay, you can HOLD him,"
K.C. grabbed my bear.
But he didn't just hold him.

He dragged my bear around by the ears,
and he fed him peanut butter,
and he tried to feed him to the dog.
Dad made him stop.

Then K.C. dragged my bear outside
where he sat on him,
and he turned the hose on him.
Dad made him stop that, too.
So K.C. buried my bear in the sand.

After K.C. went home, I dug up my bear.
Mom said, "Please, don't bring it in the house."
Dad said, "I'm sorry it's ruined, son,
but I'll buy you a new one."
I said, "I don't want a new bear.
I want this old one fixed
the way he was before K.C. came."

Mom shook her head and Dad did, too.
But Grandpa hung up his hat and he said,
"Never you mind now, Grady. I can fix that bear
so he'll be as good as new in no time."
Then he brought a big brown paper bag outside
and we sat down.

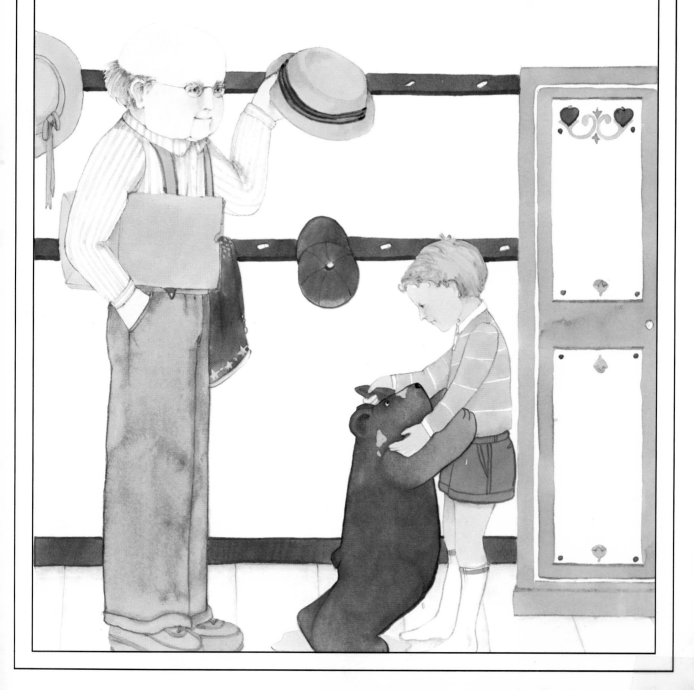

But he opened up his pocket knife!
I said, "*Wait* a minute.
What's that for, Grandpa?
Are you sure
  you can fix my bear?"
"Of course I can," he said to me.
"Hold on here and pull
  so I can see to cut the stitches."

I held on
and I pulled,
but I didn't want to watch.
Because Grandpa opened up my bear—and then—
he started pulling out the stuffing!

My bear's stomach went flat,
the way mine feels when I'm hungry.
His arms and legs wrinkled up, too,
so I said, "Grandpa, are you sure
this is the right way to fix my bear?"

Grandpa just kept on working.
My bear's nose dropped
and his head flopped,
and I covered up my eyes and I said,
"Grandpa! Are you sure?"
But he said, "Never you mind now, Grady.
We'll have this bear as good as new in no time."

In the kitchen we made a sinkful of suds
and Grandpa scrubbed my bear.
First he scrubbed the stomach,
and then the arms and legs,
and the neck and the nose,
and he even scrubbed the ears.

The water got all muddy
but my bear didn't get very clean.
"Look," I said to Grandpa.
"I can still see peanut butter."
So I pulled the plug and we made more suds,
and Grandpa scrubbed again.
But this time he scrubbed too hard.

Both the ears fell off and I said,
"Grandpa! I'm not sure
 this is the right way
 to fix my bear."
"Never you mind, now," Grandpa said.
"He'll be as good as new in no time."

Grandpa rinsed my bear
and squeezed him hard,
but when he shook him out, I told him,
"Grandpa, a clean bear's not so good
if it's all flat
and wrinkled
and it hasn't got any ears!"

"Never you mind, now," Grandpa said.
Then he hung my bear outside to dry,
with one ear on each side,
and he said, "I have to go downtown
to buy new stuffing.
Anybody want to come along?"

I did.
We rode the bus to the hobby shop.

While Grandpa bought the stuffing,
I saved his place in the popcorn line.

By the time we got back home again,
my bear and his ears were dry.
But he was still all flat and broken.
I said, "Grandpa? Are you sure…"
I guess you know what Grandpa said.

So we sat down outside again.
And Grandpa filled my bear with new fluffy stuffing.
He put about a hundred hunks of stuffing in the arms,
and he put about a hundred hunks of stuffing in the legs,
and he put about a hundred hunks of stuffing in the head,
and in the nose,
and in the neck.
But the stomach still looked hungry.
So Grandpa kept on stuffing.

Then I brought him a needle and thread and a thimble,
and he sewed the back of my bear and said, "There..."
But I said, "Wait a minute, Grandpa!
He isn't dirty anymore and he isn't flat or wrinkled, but
he still doesn't look so good without..."
"Without what? Is something missing?"
my grandpa asked, wide-eyed.

"Never you mind," he said. "I can fix that, too."
So he did. And then he said,
"There now, how does that look?"

I turned my bear all around
and carefully looked it over.
"Grandpa," I said at last,
"I thought you could fix anything.
But this bear isn't good as new."

There was a long silence
and Grandpa looked kind of sad.
"It's *better* than new!" I shouted, laughing.
And I gave him my best bear hug.

Now whenever K.C. comes to visit,
Grandpa and I grab our hats
(and my bear)
and slip out the back door,
neverminding.